A colorful adventure of

THE BEE

who left home one Monday
morning and what he found
along the way

Text copyright © 1986 by Lisa Campbell Ernst.
Illustrations copyright © 1986 by Lee Ernst.
All rights reserved. No part of this book may be reproduced or
utilized in any form or by any means, electronic or mechanical,
including photocopying, recording or by any information storage
and retrieval system, without permission in writing from the
Publisher. Inquiries should be addressed to Lothrop, Lee &
Shepard Books, a division of William Morrow & Company, Inc.,
105 Madison Avenue, New York, New York 10016.
Printed in Japan.

First Edition   1 2 3 4 5 6 7 8 9 10
Library of Congress Cataloging in Publication Data
Ernst, Lisa Campbell.
   A colorful adventure of the bee, who left home one Monday
morning and what he found along the way.
   Summary: a bee leaves its hive, passing many colors on its
route before returning home.
   [1. Bees—Fiction. 2. Stories without words. 3. Color] I. Ernst,
Lee, ill.   II. Title.   PZ7.E7323Co 1986   [E] 85-23673
ISBN 0-688-05563-X   ISBN 0-688-05564-8 (lib. bdg.)

A colorful adventure of

THE BEE

who left home one Monday
morning and what he found
along the way

by Lisa Campbell Ernst
illustrated by Lee Ernst

Lothrop, Lee & Shepard Books • New York

Dedicated to
Harriet Eyman

Yellow

Blue

Purple

Black

Green

Brown

Red

Pink

Gray

Orange

White

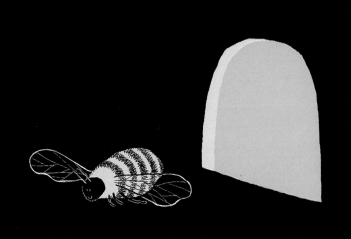